Kuma-Kuma Chan's Travels

Kazue Takahashi

MUSEYON, New York

Kuma-Kuma Chan lives in a small house deep in the mountains.

He loves to travel.

binoculars

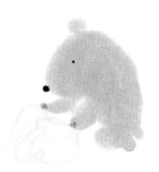

Scotch tape

chocolate

Thermos
(contains hot coffee)

bathing suit

NOTE

notebook
& pen

toothbrush
& toothpaste

sunglasses

I'd like to tell you about his travels.

Sometimes he visits a tropical island and takes a nap on the beach while listening to the waves.

Well . . . he daydreams about it.

oh

Sometimes he watches the sunrise from
the top of a mountain while drinking
a cup of fresh coffee.

Well . . . he writes about it.

The sun rises and
a pink glow covers
the mountain

Sometimes he flies high in the sky and gets
a bird's-eye view of the ground below.

Well . . . he watches the birds so that
he can learn about flying.

Sometimes Kuma-Kuma Chan gets upset and
rolls around on the ground.

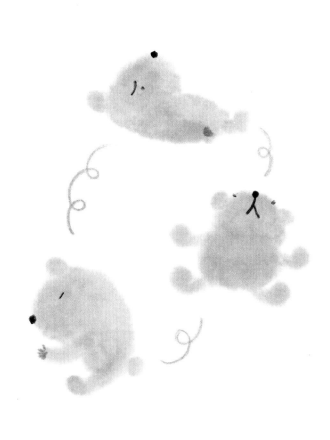

Then he calms down and takes a nap.

Sometimes he travels to a world before
he was born . . .

where he dreams he was a fierce tiger.

Sometimes he travels back in time to . . .

visit a friend he has not seen for a long time,
and they wave at each another.

Sometimes he just can't travel.

On days like that . . .

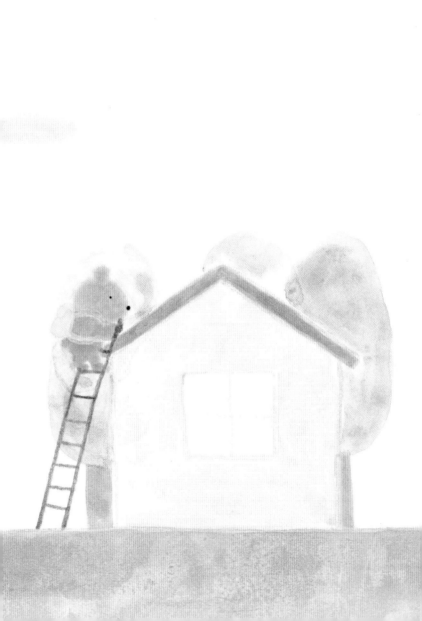

Kuma-Kuma Chan lies on his roof and
looks at the sky.

Breezes blow gently.

Clouds float past.

Birds fly by.

Eventually the sun begins to set.

When it gets dark, Kuma-Kuma Chan
listens to the . . . stars.

Kuma-Kuma Chan sends me his travel notes,
but I can't read them because . . .

he writes fast and his handwriting is messy.
So I have to imagine how his travels are going. . . .

I wonder whether he's traveling today.

Happy travels, Kuma-Kuma Chan!
See you sometime, somewhere!

Kuma-Kuma Chan's Travels

Kuma Kuma-chan, Tabi ni Deru © 2017 Kazue Takahashi

Publisher's Cataloging-in-Publication Data
Names: Takahashi, Kazue, 1971- author, illustrator. | Child, Alex, translator. | Kaplan, Simone, editor.
Title: Kuma-Kuma Chan's travels / Kazue Takahashi ; translation by Alex Child ; English editing by
Simone Kaplan.
Other titles: Kumakumachan tabi ni deru. English.
Description: New York : Museyon, [2017] | Series: Kuma-Kuma Chan ; 3 | "Originally published in
    Japan in 2017 by Poplar Publishing Co., Ltd."--Title page verso. | Audience: Age 3+. |
Identifiers: ISBN: 978-1-940842-18-9 | LCCN: 2017942132
Subjects: LCSH: Bears--Juvenile fiction. | Voyages and travels--Juvenile fiction. | Adventure and
    adventurers--Juvenile fiction. | Dreams--Juvenile fiction. | CYAC: Bears--Fiction. | Voyages
    and travels--Fiction. | Adventure and adventurers--Fiction. | Dreams--Fiction. | LCGFT:
    Picture books. | BISAC: JUVENILE FICTION / Animals / Bears.
Classification: LCC: PZ7.T14132 K86813 2017 | DDC: [E]--dc23

Published in the United States/Canada by:

Museyon Inc.
1177 Avenue of the Americas, 5th Floor
New York, NY 10036

Museyon is a registered trademark.
Visit us online at www.museyon.com

Originally published in Japan in 2017 by Poplar Publishing Co., Ltd.
English translation rights arranged with Poplar Publishing Co., Ltd.

Printed in China

ISBN 978-1-940842-18-9

0715150